DUCKLINGS

on the pond

Jan McPherson

READ BY READING

Ashton Scholastic

Auckland Sydney New York Toronto London

In springtime,
a duck went looking
for a place to make her nest.

She found a secret place
on an island
in the middle of a pond.

Quietly, she made her nest.
Secretly, she laid her eggs.
Patiently, she sat
and sat . . .

through days and nights,
through wind and rain,
keeping the precious eggs warm.

And then —

something moved inside the eggs
beneath the duck's warm belly.
Something was tapping and pecking,
tapping and pecking,
trying to get out.

On a warm spring morning
five yellow ducklings walk beside the pond.
They are now two weeks old.

The ducklings go looking for food
around the edges of the pond.

They swish their beaks around
in the muddy water.
They push their beaks under logs and stones.
The ducklings are trying to find
tiny snails and crunchy bugs to eat.

The ducklings go swimming on the pond.
They skim and skitter over the bright water,
paddling and pushing with their strong, webbed feet.

The mother duck quacks,
calling her ducklings
out of the water.

The ducklings follow her —
up the bank,
across the ditch,
over the stones,
and past the peahen . . .

Danger!
Danger for ducklings!

The tall grey peahen
comes running
at the ducklings,
running to attack them
with her sharp, pointed beak.

But the duck is ready
for the peahen's attack.

She jumps and quacks.
She fights and flaps.
She is fighting
to defend her ducklings,
and the brave mother duck
sends the peahen
hurrying away.

When all is safe once more,
the duck quacks, calling to her ducklings.

They come creeping out from their hiding places.
Then they go skidding and sliding into the water —
the calm safe water of the pond.

The day grows older.
The pond gets darker.
The ducklings are tired now —
tired of splashing and swimming
and paddling and feeding.

They need a place to sleep.

One by one,
the ducklings follow their mother
out of the water.

They climb the bank
to the island in the middle of the pond.

The duck and her ducklings will stay on the island
throughout the dark night.

When cats come creeping
and stoats come stealing,
through rain and storms
and all the dangers of the night,
the ducklings will sleep safe —

safe on their island in the middle of the pond.